Introduction

The big book of *Yeah! Chinese!* contains various resources, which provides teaching recommendations, strategies, etc. to teach each story and new words.

For teacher's convenience, the big book provides contents as following:

Story's brief introduction helps teachers be familiar with the background of each story beforehand. And teachers can differentiate teaching by expanding more information in details from students' prior knowledge.

Main characters help teachers introduce the main characters to students beforehand and guide students into the story.

Learning objectives are prepared for teachers to set up clear daily goals for students.

New words teaching guides provide teachers with suggestions on the process, strategies and activities of introducing the new words.

Warming up provides suggestions on guiding the students to predict and follow the development of the story.

Story teaching guides provide suggestions and hints to help teachers ask key points of the materials.

Hints such as teaching skills, review activities, classroom management methods, culture elements and the fun points of the stories will help teachers to prepare lessons.

Needed videos (with the logo ▶) during teaching can be found on the official website.

How to use Yeah! Chinese! to teach Chinese?

General guidelines for the procedure of a story lesson

If it is a 3 teaching periods per week, it is suggested to teach with following steps: **First period,** teach new words with song and do the activity about the targeted vocabulary. **Second period,** review the new words, song and predict the cover page of the story; and start the new story. **The last period,** do activities about the targeted vocabulary, and retell the story or do a role play. Teachers may do any changes according to class progress.

Ways to teach new words

• Teach action words such as run, catch, take, etc. with body gestures or movements. For example, when introducing the new word "run", the teacher runs at same time.

• Show the flashcards of the new words to establish meaning as an additional visual aid.

• Teach new words with most familiar songs or melodies. For example, when teaching "stand up and sit down", the teacher can sing "stand up and sit down" repeatedly with the "Ten little Indians" melody.

• Use fun activities to help students memorize new words in a low anxiety atmosphere. For example, when teaching the word "bite", ask students to walk around a circle or walk like an animal in the classroom by saying "bite".

Ways to teach story

• Prepare question word cards with Pinyin and English meaning when asking questions. When asking a question, point to the question word to establish the meaning every time.

• Introduce the main characters. e.g. He is Tom. She is Nini. Then ask students what the main characters' names are.

• Start the story from the cover. When asking questions to students, point to the question word to provide clear meaning every time. e.g. What does she say? Who is singing? Is he singing or is she dancing?

• In the middle of the story use 5-wh question words to develop or to bed the story.

• Let students predict the ending. e.g. Who feels hurt? The brother or the sister?

• Sometimes create a pause or wait time to let students finish the sentence or for a tense moment.

• Use sounds and visual tools. Capture students' attention with surprise sound effects. For example, when the students need to say "wow", teach them to use funny sound effect for "wow".

• Maintain eye contact. It will draw students' attention when the teacher makes eye contact with them.

• Use multiple ways of movement. For example, when the students hear the new words such as "be quiet", they need to show "quiet" gesture. As the storyteller, the teacher can "paint" pictures with his / her hands, feet, legs and head.

• Change your voice with different characters. Voice is one of the best ways to bring the character to life and gets students' attention immediately.

• Use props. Don't introduce the props all at once, but bring them out one by one during poignant parts in the telling.

Ways to teach song

• Slow & body movements are the key methods to teach song.

• First of all, let students listen to the melody by demonstrating with body movement.

• The teacher demonstrates singing the song line by line slowly.

• Invite students as a song leader to guide others for singing.

• Sing fast or slow, higher or lower for fun. Let students sing very slowly or sing faster each time to exaggerate the tempo.

• Humming the song. When students are familiar with the song, let them hum the song, which make the song more attractive for them to sing.

• Magic claps or stamp feet. When hearing assigned words, students need to clap hands or "be quiet" or stamp feet. After couple time of practices, then have a competition.

• Play games when singing a song.

Ways to teach games

- Games are played in very class period as a review for the language.
- Model the game before it starts. Invite one or two students to demonstrate how to play the game.
- Explain teacher's expectations before the games.
- Prepare the props or flashcards beforehand for the games.

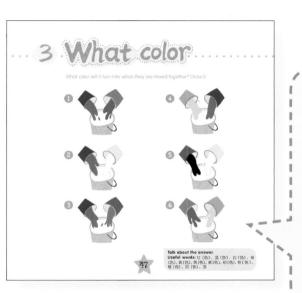

How to use activities

- Activities are designed to reinforce students' speaking and listening skills.
- Model before starting the activity.
- Prepare the activities with diversified requirements to achieve the maximum benefit of the activity.
- Provide students with more practice in the process by having them share the answers with their partners before answering the class.

Ways to retell a story / do a role play

- Pair up students to retell the story with the retelling page.
- Pair up students. When a student describes the picture randomly, another one points to the picture accordingly.
- Invite students to act out the story either with props or character cards.
- Let students use props or a stage theater to retell the story or do a role play which help some students who are shy to present in low anxiety.

How to use word list

Students themselves can use the word list to review and monitor what they have learned after class. The teacher can use it to check if the students have mastered the words or not. A better way of checking is to combine the word list with flashcards. For example, students should find the correct flashcard when the teacher says a word at random.

Contents

Word list

故事简介

小动物们在服装店里试衣服。小鸡、长颈鹿和小熊都看上了同一件衣服。小鸡穿上太大了，长颈鹿穿上太短了，小熊穿上不长不短正合适，但是正当小熊高兴的时候，它的小肚子把衣服扣子撑掉了。

教学目标

1.掌握常用动词"穿"。
2.掌握常用名词"衣服"和"扣子"。

主要人物

小鸡

长颈鹿

小熊

生词教学

• 穿

1. 领读。（展示图片或动作演示。）
2. 观看视频 ，让学生说一说视频中的人物在做什么。
3. 准备两个大玩偶，让学生分组比赛，帮助玩偶穿衣服，哪一组穿得又快又好，哪一组就赢了。

• 衣服

1. 领读。（展示图片。）
2. 准备不同颜色衣服的图片，让学生说一说他们喜欢穿什么颜色的衣服。
3. 借助课本 P10 的游戏练习词语。

小提示

和"脱""衣服"一起教。

小提示

和"穿""脱"一起教。

New words

- 穿
  put on; wear
- 衣服
  clothes
- 扣子
  button

学过的词： 小鸡、长颈鹿、小熊、掉了

- 扣子
1. 领读。（展示图片。）
2. 借助课本 P9 的歌曲练习词语。
3. 借助课本 P12 的活动练习词语。

故事热身

提问

1. 你看到什么动物？（让学生说一说。）
2. 大家在哪里？（让学生说一说。）
3. 小鸡喜欢哪件衣服？这件衣服什么颜色？（让学生说一说。）

小提示

1. 借助书中的人物图介绍故事主要人物: 小鸡、长颈鹿和小熊。
2. 教师准备英文图卡解释可能用到的、学生没学过的词语。
3. 提示学生注意动物们的表情和动作，让学生说一说它们要做什么。

小鸡穿衣服。

提问

1. 小鸡在做什么？（指着小鸡问。）

2. 衣服大吗？（指着衣服问。）

3. 长颈鹿为什么笑了？（让学生说一说。）

小提示

1. 提示学生注意小鸡的表情，让学生说一说它怎么了。

2. 提示学生注意长颈鹿的表情和动作，让学生说一说发生了什么。

提问

1. 长颈鹿在做什么？（指着长颈鹿问。）
2. 衣服短不短？（指着衣服问。）
3. 小熊为什么笑了？（指着小熊问。）

小提示

1. 提示学生注意长颈鹿的表情，让学生说一说它怎么了。
2. 提示学生注意小熊的表情和动作，让学生说一说发生了什么。

提问

1. 小熊在做什么？（指着小熊问。）
2. 小熊喜欢它的衣服吗？（指着小熊问。）
3. 衣服有几个扣子？（指着衣服问。）

小提示

提示学生注意长颈鹿和小鸡的表情，让学生说一说它们可能说什么。

提问

1. 小熊妈妈说什么？（指着小熊妈妈问。）
2. 小熊妈妈为什么说"哎呀"？（指着小熊妈妈问。）

小提示

1. 提示学生注意观察小熊的背影，让学生猜一猜发生了什么。
2. 提示学生注意长颈鹿和小鸡的表情，让学生猜一猜它们想说什么。

提问

1. 扣子怎么了？（指着扣子问。）
2. 扣子为什么掉了？（指着扣子问，让学生说一说。）

小提示

提示学生注意观察小熊妈妈、长颈鹿和小鸡的表情和动作，让学生说一说它们为什么笑。

我的裤子
My trousers

故事简介

小动物们在游乐场里玩儿。河马、小猪和小熊滑滑梯。河马去挑战最高的滑梯，它爬到最高的地方滑下来，结果裤子破了。

教学目标

1. 掌握常用词语"滑滑梯"。
2. 认识动物"河马"。
3. 掌握常用名词"裤子"。
4. 学生能用"破了"描述状态。

主要人物

河马

小猪

小熊

生词教学

• 滑滑梯

1.领读。（展示图片。）

2.观看视频 ▶ ，让学生说一说视频中的动物、人物在玩儿什么。

3.借助课本 P21 的歌曲练习词语。

小提示

在确认安全的前提下，老师可以带学生到学校游乐场滑滑梯。

• 河马

1.领读。（展示图片。）

2.观看视频 ▶ ，问问学生喜不喜欢河马。

小提示

1.带领学生复习学过的动物名词。

2.让学生画一画河马。

New words

- 滑滑梯
  slide
- 河马
  hippo
- 裤子
  trousers
- 破了
  worn out

学过的词：小熊、小猪

- **裤子**
1. 领读。（展示图片。）
2. 准备不同颜色裤子的图片，让学生说一说他们喜欢穿什么颜色的裤子。
3. 借助课本 P24 的活动练习词语。

- **破了**
1. 领读。（展示图片。）
2. 借助课本 P23 的活动练习词语。

故事热身

提问

1. 你看到什么动物？（让学生说一说。）
2. 你想滑哪个滑梯？（让学生说一说。）

小提示

1. "找衣服和裤子"比赛：准备一些裤子和衣服的图片，然后将学生分组，让学生听指令找衣服和裤子。例如，老师说"我要穿绿色的裤子和蓝色的衣服"，然后每组同学就去找，哪组在最短时间内找到，哪组就赢了。
2. 可以带领学生复习"穿""脱"和"衣服"。

小提示

1. 借助书中的人物图介绍故事主要人物：河马、小猪和小熊。
2. 教师准备英文图卡解释可能用到的、学生没学过的词语。

Story

小熊滑滑梯。

提问

1. 小熊在做什么？（指着小熊问。）
2. 滑梯什么样子？（指着滑梯问。）
3. 你喜欢滑滑梯吗？（让学生说一说。）

小提示

提示学生注意小猪的表情和动作，让学生说一说它想去做什么。

小猪滑滑梯。

提问

1. 小猪在做什么？（指着小猪问。）

2. 小猪喜欢滑滑梯吗？（让学生说一说。）

3. 小猪滑的滑梯高还是小熊滑的滑梯高？（让学生说一说。）

河马滑滑梯。

提问

1. 滑梯高不高？（指着滑梯问。）
2. 河马厉害吗？（指着河马问。）

小提示

提示学生注意小熊的表情和动作，让学生说一说小熊想说什么。

提问

小熊和小猪说什么？为什么这样说？（指着小熊和小猪问。）

小提示

提示学生观察小熊和小猪的表情和动作，让学生猜一猜发生了什么。

提问

1. 河马的裤子怎么了？（指着河马的裤子问。）

2. 小熊为什么闭眼睛？（指着小熊问。）

3. 小猪想说什么？（指着小猪问。）

小提示

提示学生观察小熊、小猪和河马的表情和动作，让学生说一说河马的裤子为什么破了。

Lesson 3
我的鞋子
My shoes

故事简介

Aiko、Alan、Bobo 和 Tom 去参加派对。他们盛装出席，都穿了新鞋子，非常开心。Tom 穿了一双雨鞋，他着急赶来展示自己的雨鞋，一脚踩到了水里，水溅到了大家的新鞋子上。

教学目标

1. 掌握颜色词语"棕（色）"和"灰（色）"。
2. 掌握常用名词"鞋子"和"雨鞋"。

主要人物

Aiko

Alan

Bobo

Tom

生词教学

● **棕（色）**

1. 领读。（展示图片。）
2. 观看视频 ▶，让学生说一说视频中有什么颜色。

● **灰（色）**

1. 领读。（展示图片。）
2. 观看视频 ▶，让学生说一说视频中有什么颜色。
3. 借助课本 P34 的游戏练习词语。

小提示

颜色"小调查"：准备有关颜色的调查问卷，让学生互相访问他们对颜色（包括"棕色"和"灰色"）的喜好。

小提示

准备各种颜色（包括"棕色"和"灰色"）的动物图片，然后将学生分组，每组学生要在规定时间内找出含有目标颜色的动物图片，并要大声说出是什么动物。哪组找得多，哪组就赢了。

New words

- 棕（色）
  brown
- 灰（色）
  grey
- 鞋子
  shoes
- 雨鞋
  rain boots

学过的词：穿、红色

- **鞋子**

1. 领读。（展示图片。）
2. 观看视频 ▶ ，让学生说一说喜欢什么颜色的鞋子。
3. 借助课本 P35 和 P36 的活动练习词语。

故事热身

提问

1. 他们去哪里？（让学生观察图片说一说。）
2. 他们为什么拿着礼物？（指着 Aiko、Alan、Bobo 和 Tom 问，让学生猜一猜。）
3. 他们穿什么颜色的衣服？他们的衣服好看吗？（指着 Aiko、Alan、Bobo 和 Tom 问。）

- **雨鞋**

1. 领读。（展示图片。）
2. 观看视频 ▶ ，让学生说一说下雨要穿什么。
3. 借助课本 P33 的歌曲练习词语。

小提示

1. 借助书中的人物图介绍故事主要人物：Aiko、Alan、Bobo 和 Tom。
2. 教师准备英文图卡解释可能用到的、学生没学过的词语。
3. 提示学生注意刚刚下过雨，地上有水。

Story

Aiko 穿红色的鞋子。

提问

1. Aiko 穿什么颜色的鞋子？（指着 Aiko 问。）
2. Bobo 喜欢 Aiko 红色的鞋子吗？（指着 Bobo 问。）
3. 你喜欢穿红色的鞋子吗？（让学生说一说。）

小提示

提示学生注意 Bobo 的表情和手势，让学生猜一猜 Bobo 想对 Aiko 说什么。

提问

1. Alan 穿什么颜色的鞋子?（指着 Alan 问。）
2. 谁喜欢 Alan 棕色的鞋子?（让学生说一说。）
3. 你穿什么颜色的鞋子?（让学生说一说。）

小提示

1. 提示学生注意 Alan 的表情和手势，让学生说一说 Alan 是不是非常喜欢自己的鞋子。
2. 提示学生注意 Bobo 的表情和手势，让学生猜一猜 Bobo 想对 Alan 说什么。

提问

1. Bobo 穿什么颜色的鞋子？（指着 Bobo 问。）

2. 谁喜欢穿灰色的鞋子？（让学生说一说。）

3. 老师（指着自己）穿什么颜色的鞋子？（让学生说一说。）

小提示

提示学生注意 Alan 的表情和手势，让学生说一说 Alan 是不是也喜欢 Bobo 灰色的鞋子。

提问

1. Tom 说什么？（指着 Tom 问。）
2. Tom 的雨鞋什么颜色？（指着 Tom 问。）
3. 你下雨天穿什么？（让学生说一说。）

提问

1. Aiko 为什么说"哎呀"？（指着 Aiko 问。）
2. Tom 看到地面上有水了吗？（指着 Tom 问。）

小提示

1. 提示学生注意 Aiko、Alan、Bobo 和 Tom 的表情，让学生说一说发生了什么。
2. 雨天穿雨鞋好还是穿普通鞋子好？让学生说一说。

穿裙子
Wear a dress

故事简介

Nini 准备去参加 Helen 的生日派对，在衣柜前面挑选衣服。奶奶和妈妈选的裙子 Nini 都不喜欢。她自己选了一条白色的裙子，可是不小心碰洒了妈妈手里的咖啡，咖啡洒到了裙子上。

教学目标

1. 掌握颜色词语"粉（色）"和"橙（色）"。
2. 掌握常用名词"裙子"。
3. 学生能用"好看"描述状态。

主要人物

Nini

奶奶

妈妈

生词教学

• 粉（色）

1. 领读。（展示图片。）

2. 观看视频 ▶，让学生说一说视频中有什么颜色。

3. 借助课本 P45 的歌曲练习词语。

• 橙（色）

1. 领读。（展示图片。）

2. 观看视频 ▶，让学生说一说视频中有什么颜色。

3. 借助课本 P47 的活动练习词语。

• 裙子

1. 领读。（展示图片。）

2. 借助课本 P48 的活动练习词语。

• 好看

1. 领读。

2. 准备各种衣服、鞋子的图片，让学生说一说好看不好看。

New words

- 粉（色）
  pink
- 橙（色）
  orange
- 裙子
  dress
- 好看
  pretty

学过的词： 奶奶、妈妈、我、白色、漂亮

故事热身

提问

1. Nini 的衣柜里有什么颜色的裙子？（指着 Nini 的衣柜问。）
2. 奶奶和妈妈的衣服什么颜色？（指着奶奶和妈妈的衣服问。）
3. 谁过生日？（指着生日卡问。）

小提示

1. 借助书中的人物图介绍故事主要人物：Nini、奶奶和妈妈。
2. 教师准备英文图卡解释可能用到的、学生没学过的词语。
3. 提示学生注意衣柜里的衣服，让学生猜一猜 Nini 想穿什么。

Story

粉色的裙子
好看。

提问

1. 奶奶说什么？（指着奶奶问。）
2. Nini 身上的衣服什么颜色？（指着 Nini 的衣服问。）
3. 粉色的裙子好看还是红色的裙子好看？（让学生说一说。）

小提示

提示学生注意 Nini 的表情和动作，让学生说一说她喜不喜欢奶奶拿的裙子。

橙色的裙子
好看。

提问

1.妈妈说什么？（指着妈妈问。）

2.奶奶喜欢橙色的裙子吗？（指着奶奶问。）

小提示

1. 提示学生注意 Nini 的表情和动作，让学生猜一猜她会不会穿橙色的裙子。

2. 提示学生注意奶奶的表情和动作，让学生猜一猜她想说什么。

提问

1. Nini 说什么？（指着 Nini 问。）

2. 你喜欢穿裙子吗？你喜欢什么颜色的裙子？（让学生说一说。）

我漂亮吗？

提问

1. Nini 说什么？（指着 Nini 问。）

2. 妈妈手里拿着什么？（让学生猜一猜。）

3. 桌子上面放着什么？（指着桌子问。）

小提示

1. 提示学生注意 Nini 的动作，让学生猜一猜会发生什么。

2. 提示学生注意妈妈和奶奶的表情和动作，让学生说一说妈妈和奶奶喜不喜欢 Nini 的裙子。

提问

1. Nini 的裙子怎么了？（指着 Nini 的裙子问。）
2. 奶奶为什么站起来了？（指着奶奶问。）

小提示

提示学生注意 Nini 的表情和动作，让学生说一说发生了什么。